For Maddy, Phoebe, Willa, Fenner, Sophie, and Sam
—C. S.

To my wife, Nancy, who has opened many doors for me
—L. C.

KNOCK
KNOCK

Once there was an old man and old woman who lived on a farm along a lonely road. One cold, snowy night they heard a KNOCK, KNOCK, KNOCK at the door.

Who's Knocking at the Door?

Carla Stevens
illustrated by Lee Chapman

Marshall Cavendish
New York • London
Singapore

Marshall Cavendish, 99 White Plains Road, Tarrytown, NY 10591
www.marshallcavendish.com

Library of Congress Cataloging-in-Publication Data
Stevens, Carla.
Who's knocking at the door? / by Carla Stevens ; illustrated by Lee
Chapman.— 1st ed.
p. cm.
Summary: An elderly farm couple gives shelter to a talking horse,
a cow, and two hens on a cold night, and, in gratitude,
the animals save them from two robbers.
ISBN 0-7614-5168-4
[1. Old age—Fiction. 2. Domestic animals—Fiction. 3.
Kindness--Fiction.] I. Title: Who is knocking at the door?. II.
Chapman, Lee, ill. III. Title.
PZ7.S8435Wh 2004
[E]—dc22
2003020299

The text of this book is set in Slappy Inline.
The illustrations are rendered in oil paint on canvas
with the occasional animal hair mixed in.

Printed in China
First edition
1 3 5 6 4 2

"Who can be out on a night like this?"
the old woman asked.

"We'll soon find out," her husband said.
And he went to the door and opened it.

A horse stood in the doorway.
"I've come a long way, and I'm very tired,"
he said. "Could you put me up for the night?"

"Make yourself at home," the old man replied.
"But please close the door. It's cold out."

"Thank you," said the horse. He walked to a corner of the room—CLIPPITY CLOP, CLIPPITY CLOP— and stood quietly, looking out the window.

The old man sat down at the kitchen table. "Wife," he whispered. "Have you ever heard a horse talk before?"

"No," the old woman replied, as she passed a slice of apple pie to her husband. "But there's a first time for everything."

Just then they heard another knock at the door. The old man sighed. "If it isn't one thing, it's another." And he got up and opened the door.

Two fat hens fluttered and flapped in the doorway.
"O-o-o-o-o-h. It's much too cold to roost in a tree tonight.
May we take shelter with you, please?"

"Come in, come in," the old man said. "You can roost near
the fireplace."

So the hens flew—FLIPPITY FLAPPITY—to the fireplace.
When the old man returned to the table, he whispered,
"Wife, whoever heard of a talking hen?"

The old woman smiled at her husband.
"If a horse can talk, why not a hen?"

What a cozy spot
this is, Mabel.

FLIPPITY
FLAPPITY

Oops!
I just laid an egg!

Just as they were drying the last supper dish, they heard yet another knock on the door.
"I hope it isn't a cow this time," the old man said.
But it was.

"I can't walk another step," said the cow, groaning. "My hooves are killing me. Please let me stay with you tonight."

"There's always room for one more," said the old man, opening the door wide.

"Thank you." The cow stepped inside, and when she saw the horse, she exclaimed, "Thank goodness you're here!"

And she went CLUMPITY CLUMP, CLUMPITY CLUMP across the room until she stood beside him.

It was late and the old man and old woman were tired, so they went upstairs to bed. The next morning, when they woke up, they heard voices in the kitchen below. And when they went downstairs, they found the cow sweeping the floor, the hens cooking pancakes on the stove, and the horse carrying in wood for the fire.

"Breakfast is ready. Please sit down," said the hens.

So the old man and the old woman sat down at the table with their guests, and while eating many pancakes, they talked about many things.

At last the horse said, "You were very kind to give us shelter. Now we must be off."

After thanking the old man and woman, the four animals went on their way.

"I never thought that a horse, a cow, and two hens could be such good company," said the old man.

"Looks can be deceiving," his wife replied, as she put the maple syrup back in the cupboard.

Suddenly they heard a loud knocking at the door.

"They must have forgotten something," the old man said.
But when he opened the door, he saw a man
with a coil of rope in one hand and a cage in the other.

"Where are my animals?" the farmer shouted.

"Your animals?" the old man asked.

"Yes!" shouted the farmer. "I see tracks all around the outside
of your house."

"They left early this morning," said the old man. "But they
didn't tell us where they were going."

"And of course we were too polite to ask," added his wife.

"You silly old woman! Of course they didn't tell you! Animals can't talk!"

And off went the farmer, muttering to himself, "Just wait 'til I get my hands on those lazy, good-for-nothing beasts!"

"Good riddance!" the old woman said, as she slammed the door.

Then they spent the rest of the day, like so many others, cooking and cleaning, eating and napping, and playing game after game of checkers.

Your move.

At last it was time to go to bed.
Suddenly two men carrying bags pushed open the front door.
"Get out of our way, old man and old woman!
And don't you dare come back until we tell you to!"

"If it isn't one thing, it's another, Wife,"
muttered the old man, and they hurried upstairs.

"What can they be doing down there?" whispered the old woman, jumping into bed.

"Something not good," whispered the old man, as they hid under the covers.

They listened to the gruff voices of the two men and the clinking of coins until they fell asleep.

The next morning, when they awoke, they heard the clatter of dishes.

"I smell something cooking," said the old woman.

"I hope those men are feeling better this morning," said the old man.

"Me too," the old woman said. "I'm hungry."

So they went down the stairs very, very cautiously. And guess who they saw in the kitchen?

Heh heh!

Mmm!

"Good morning," the cow said. "Are you surprised to see us again?"

"Oh yes," the old man exclaimed. "Last night two men were here."

"We know," the horse said. "They're still here. We have locked them in your closet."

"They are robbers," the hens added. "When they passed us yesterday, we heard them talking about stopping here, so we came back to be sure they did you no harm."

"One good turn deserves another," said the cow. "Here are the bags of money they stole."

The old woman picked up a bag.
"Oh, my!" she exclaimed. "This bag is heavy!"

Just then they heard a KNOCK, KNOCK, KNOCK.

"We haven't had so much company in years," the old man said, as he opened the door.

A tall man wearing a big hat held out a badge.
"I am—I am—well, to make a long story short, I am the sheriff. I'm looking for—Who AM I looking for?" he asked, removing his hat to scratch his head.

"Robbers, perhaps?" suggested the old man.

"Robbers! You're right. Two robbers!"

The old woman pointed. "They're in the closet."

"Why are they in the closet? Oh, I know!
They must be hanging up their coats," said the sheriff.

Let me out!

Any more excitement,
and I'll lay another egg!

The sheriff opened the door.
BANG, BOOM, KERPLUNK.
Out fell the robbers.
"Just wait 'til we get our hands on that talking horse!"
they shouted.

"Hands—hands—oh, I almost forgot. Handcuffs!"

And the sheriff quickly pulled two pairs of handcuffs
out of his pocket and put them on the robbers.
CLICK CLACK, CLICK CLACK.

"Here's the money they stole!" said the old woman.
And she handed him the bags of money.

"Money? Money? Oh, I almost forgot.
You get a reward for catching the robbers."
The sheriff opened a bag, counted fifty dollars,
and gave the money to the old woman.

"HI HO, HI HO!" sang the sheriff.
"It's off to jail we go!"
But just as he and the robbers
were leaving, the farmer
appeared again.

"Aha!" he shouted. "There
they are!"

"Oh, no you don't!" yelled
the sheriff. "I got here first!
These are MY robbers."
And he pushed the robbers
out the door.

SQUAWK

The farmer went over to the cow and pulled her tail.
"You lazy, good-for-nothing cow!"

"**MOOO, MOOO**," the cow said.

"And you! You stupid old horse!"
He turned to the horse and kicked him.

"**NEIGHHH, NEIGHHH!**" the horse said.

Then the farmer tried to catch the clucking hens,
but they flew up onto the rafters.

"I'll teach you a lesson. It's off to market you all go!"

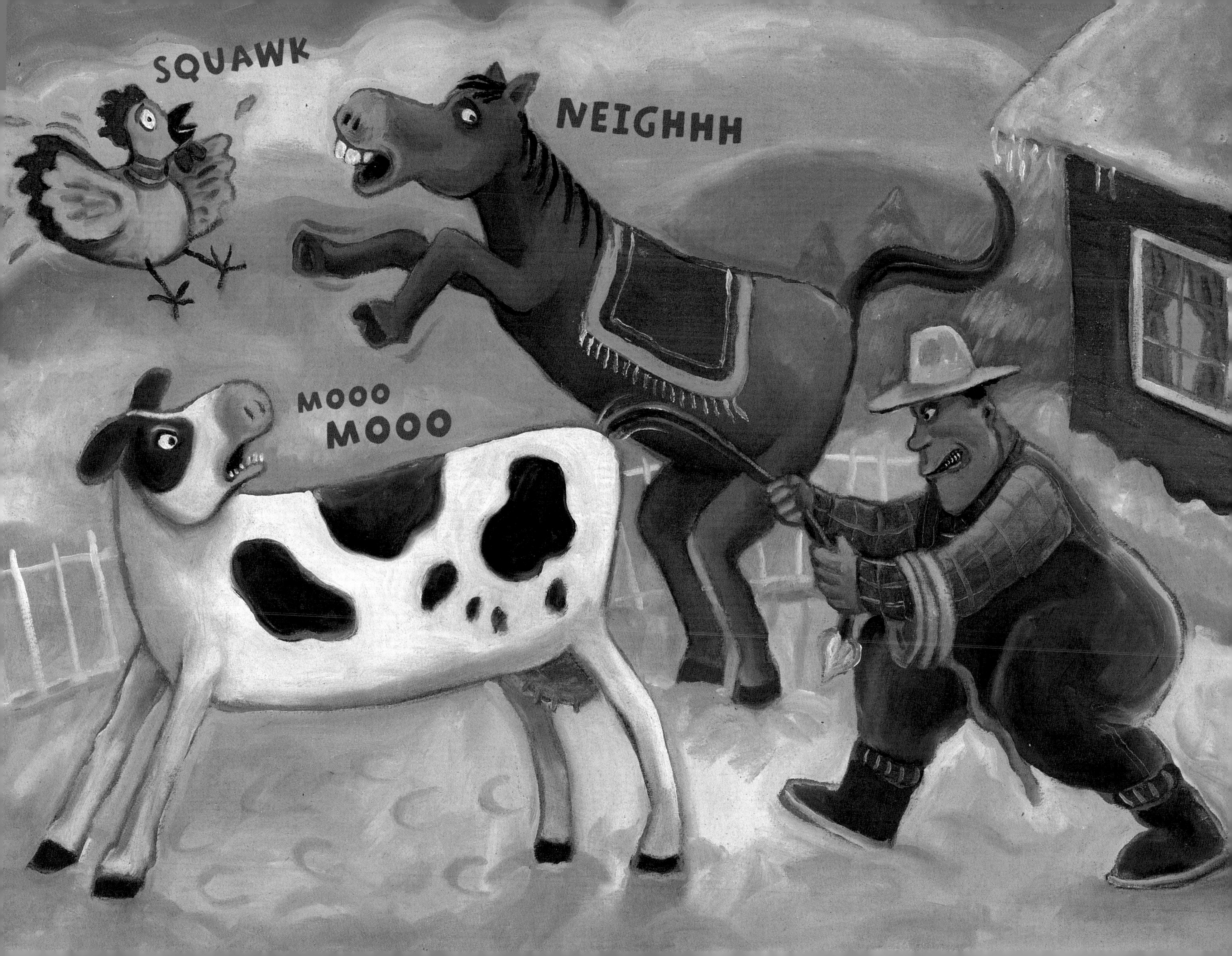
SQUAWK
NEIGHHH
MOOO
MOOO

"Wait!" the old woman cried. "There is no need to take your animals to market. We'll buy them from you."

"You can have them for fifty dollars," the farmer said. "I won't take a penny less."

The old woman smiled. "You drive a hard bargain," she said, as she gave him the money.

So the farmer went away counting—"Forty-one, forty-two, forty-three, forty-four . . ."

And very soon after, the horse and the cow and the hens began to dance a jig. Then the old man and the old woman were dancing too.

And that's the end of the story, except to tell you that they all lived together, enjoying the good company of one another for many years to come.

All is well that ends well!